Rainbow Brite™

Starlite and Twink

By Ellie O'Ryan

Illustration by Carol Haantz

Scholastic Reader — Level 3

ISBN 0-439-66790-9

RAINBOW BRITE™ © 2004 Hallmark Licensing, Inc.
Used under license by Scholastic Inc. All rights reserved. Published by Scholastic Inc.
SCHOLASTIC and associated logos are trademarks and/or registered trademarks of Scholastic Inc.

12 11 10 9 8 7 6 5 4 3 2   4 5 6 7 8/0

Printed in the U.S.A.
First printing, September 2004

SCHOLASTIC INC.

New York Toronto London Auckland Sydney
Mexico City New Delhi Hong Kong Buenos Aires

Rainbow Brite needed help.
It was time to check the colors.
"I'll help," said Twink.
"No, I will," said Starlite.
"I'm stronger and faster."
"Says who?" asked Twink.

"You can both help me,"
said Rainbow Brite.
"First we need a pail
to carry the Star Sprinkles."
"I'll get it!" Starlite said.
"No, I'll get it!" said Twink.

"Thanks, Starlite,"
Rainbow Brite said.
"Now I need
my color belt."
"I've got it!" said Twink.
"I can get it!" said Starlite.

"Thanks, Twink,"
said Rainbow Brite.
"Now we just need the map."
"I'll go get it!" said Twink.
"No, I want to get it!" said Starlite.

Oh, no!
Starlite and Twink
ripped the map!

Starlite was very mad.
"You ripped the map!"
he yelled at Twink.

Twink got mad back.
"I did not!" he yelled.
"And I called it first!"

Rainbow Brite did not want
her two best friends to fight.
She tried to help them make up.

"Please don't fight," she said.
"It was a mistake.
Friends are friends
no matter what."

"I'm sorry," said Twink.
"I'm sorry, too," said Starlite.
"We both ripped the map," Twink said.
"And we can both fix it!" Starlite said.

Starlite got the tape.
Twink put the pieces together.

"That's more like it!"
said Rainbow Brite.
"Now let's go check
the colors!"

Rainbow Brite took red Star Sprinkles to Red Region.

She dropped orange Star Sprinkles on Orange Meadows.

Rainbow Brite used
yellow Star Sprinkles
in Yellow Plains.

She brightened
Green Grange
with green
Star Sprinkles.

Rainbow Brite brought
blue Star Sprinkles
to Blue Zone.

She made Indigo Acres brighter
with indigo Star Sprinkles.

And Rainbow Brite spread
violet Star Sprinkles
all over Violet Valley!

Rainbow Land was full of
bright colors and best friends —
just the way Rainbow Brite liked it!